The Book of Conflictius

By

Dumaine Landa

Dedicated to

Zaine and Zaiba

Love Dad

Table of Contents

VERSE I ____ 1

VERSE II ____ 2

VERSE III ____ 3

VERSE IV ____ 4

VERSE V ____ 5

VERSE VI ____ 6

VERSE VII ____ 7

VERSE VIII _______________________________________ 8

VERSE IX ____ 9

VERSE X ____ 10

VERSE XI ____ 11

VERSE XII _______________________________________ 12

VERSE XIII _______________________________________ 13

VERSE XIV _______________________________________ 14

VERSE XV ____ 15

VERSE XVI _______________________________________ 16

VERSE XVII ______________________________________ 17

VERSE XVIII _____________________________________ 18

VERSE XIX _______________________________________ 19

VERSE XX ____ 20

VERSE XXI _______________________________________ 21

VERSE XXII ______________________________________ 22

VERSE XXIII ______________________________________ 23

VERSE XXIV _____________________________________ 24

VERSE XXV ______________________________________ 25

VERSE XXVI _____________________________________ 26

VERSE XXVII ____ 27

VERSE XXVIII____ 28

VERSE XXIX ____ 29

VERSE XXX ____ 30

VERSE XXXI ____ 31

VERSE XXXII ____ 32

VERSE XXXIII ____ 33

VERSE XXXIV____ 34

VERSE XXXV ____ 35

VERSE XXXVI____ 36

VERSE XXXVII____ 37

VERSE XXXVIII____ 38

VERSE XXXIX ____ 39

VERSE XL ____ 40

VERSE XLI ____ 41

VERSE I

AWARENESS

IS THE

KEY!!!!!

VERSE II

LEARN OR BURN

Mistakes are made

to be Learnt from

VERSE III

If you do not LEARN

From Mistakes

The lesson will be Repeated

Until You Do

VERSE IV

ACTION SPEAKS LOUDER

THAN WORDS.

A person is to be Judged by their ACTIONS

and not by their WORDS

5

VERSE V

You may Not Know What You Want.

But Surely You Know

What You Do Not Want

VERSE VI

Life is an ILLUSION which

YOU MUST CONTROL

or else it will

CONTROL YOU!!!!!

VERSE VII

You must CONTROL

Your

OWN MIND

or else it

will CONTROL YOU!!!!!

VERSE VIII

BALANCE

IS

FUNDAMENTAL

VERSE IX

BALANCE is the

route to WHOLENESS

Be ONE with ALL!!!!!

VERSE X

RECIPROCATION

Is the

Foundation of Relations

VERSE XI

NEVER REACT WITH

EMOTIONS

EMOTIONS ARE THE ENEMY

OF BALANCE

VERSE XII

When You Don't Know

What to Do?!?!?

DO NOTHING!!!!!

Always be fully sure

Of your CHOICES

VERSE XIII

GOD SEES ALL!!!!!

ULTIMATELY IT IS

YOUR THOUGHTS

AND

CHOICES

THAT DEFINES

YOUR PRESENT AND FUTURE

VERSE XIV

THOUGHTS ARE FREQUENCIES

FREQUENCIES AFFECT

OUR WHOLE BEING!!!!!

VERSE XV

INTERNAL DIALOGUE

COULD BE A MULTIPLEX!!!!!

Like a bundle of

Tangled wires!!!!!

The wires must be

UNTANGLED

One at a time

For Peace of Mind

VERSE XVI

In order to be able to THINK

With CLARITY and without

INFLUENCE

One must keep the Mind

Focused on one THOUGHT

VERSE XVII

Sometimes the battle to

CONTROL YOUR OWN THOUGHTS

Is like fighting an

INVISIBLE OPPONENT

VERSE XVIII

In order to fight an

INVISIBLE OPPONENT

You must use your SENSES

To sedate It!!!!!

VERSE XIX

In order to formulate

A counter-attack

You may first have to

Endure all

Of your opponent's attacks

In order to learn their

MOVES AND PATTERNS

VERSE XX

When a PATTERN is apparent

Then a PREDICTION

Can be formed based on that

PATTERN

VERSE XXI

Before a PROBLEM

Can be solved

You must first

Know exactly

What the PROBLEM is

in as much

Detail as possible

VERSE XXII

Sometimes UNDERSTANDING

A PROBLEM

Is the Route to the

SOLUTION

23

VERSE XXIII

EVERYBODY HAS TRIGGERS!!!!!

VERSE XXIV

Become AWARE

Of all your

TRIGGERS!!!!!

And any associated

Habits or Behaviour!!!!!

VERSE XXV

When you are AWARE of

Your TRIGGERS!!!!!

Then be AWARE not to

REACT!!!!!

VERSE XXVI

IF SOMEONE KNOWS

YOUR TRIGGERS!!!!!

AND KEEPS ON

TRIGGERING YOU!!!!!

THEY MAY NOT NECESSARILY BE

YOUR ENEMY

THEY MAY BE YOUR HEALER

VERSE XXVII

The Healer will Keep

On TRIGGERING You

Until You Attain

AWARENESS

VERSE XXVIII

The Healer May Not

Be What You

Perceive…!!!!!

29

VERSE XXIX

The Healer Maybe

In Need of

Healing…!!!!!

VERSE XXX

Avoiding TRIGGERS Does Not

Neutralise Them.

With AWARENESS and BALANCE

You must Expose Yourself

To Your TRIGGERS

And Learn Not

To REACT…!!!!!

VERSE XXXI

Boundaries are a Necessity.

Toxic Beings and Energy

Must be Confined…!!!!!

VERSE XXXII

Don't Expect Society

To Respect

Your TRIGGERS and BOUNDERIES…!!!!!

VERSE XXXIII

Your TRIGGERS and BOUNDARIES

Are Your Responsibility…!!!!!

VERSE XXXIV

Choose your battles Wisely

A KING does not REACT

To a Peasant

VERSE XXXV

The difference between a

WARRIOR and a Fighter is

Like a HUNTER, the WARRIOR

Knows when to Strike

ALWAYS RESERVE ENERGY!!!!!

VERSE XXXVI

When battling

with your THOUGHTS

or a

INVISIBLE ENEMY

Remember to

Take Breaks

VERSE XXXVII

Information is POWER

Only to be Disclosed

When Necessary…!!!!!

VERSE XXXVIII

To have great POWER

You must know when

To REACT

In CHESS the KING

Is only Moved out of

NECCESSITY…!!!!!

VERSE XXXIX

WITH POWER COMES

GREAT RESPONSIBILITY

The more ENLIGHTENED

You become

The harder the Devil

Will try to Seduce

YOUR MIND WITH TEMPTATION

VERSE XL

To find Heaven in hell

Is to attain TRUE HAPPINESS

Which cannot be

STOLEN NOR BOUGHT!!!!!

VERSE XLI

OM IS ONE WITH ALL!!!!!

BE ONE WITH OM